Wher Dinosaurs Walked

Isabel Thomas

Illustrated by Lexie Mac

Schofield & Sims

Long ago, our planet was hotter and wetter.

Land animals grew bigger than they do today.

Stegosaurus tore through forests like tanks!

Dinosaurs were the biggest animals ever to walk on land.

Allosaurus was one of the biggest carnivores.

sharp teeth

huge claws

Dinosaurs were not the only prehistoric giants. Our planet was once home to massive creepy crawlies too.

Let's explore and find out more!

This prehistoric cockroach lived long before the dinosaurs.

size of a prehistoric cockroach

Its jaws could bore through wood as thick as a door!

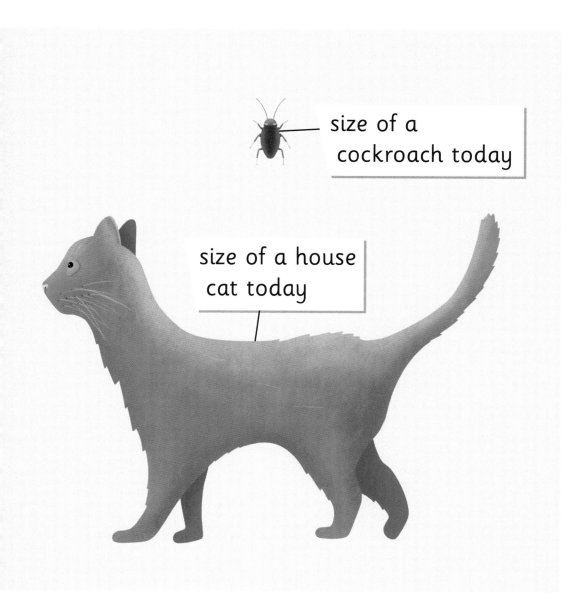

size of a cockroach today

size of a house cat today

The biggest insect in history was a giant dragonfly.

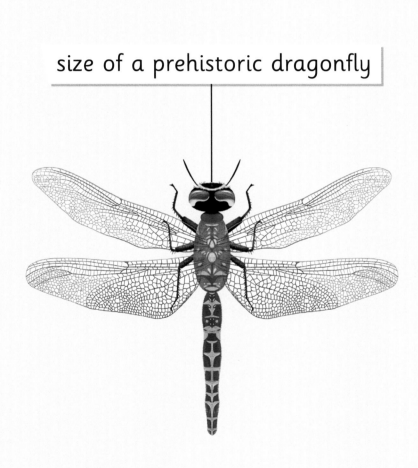

size of a prehistoric dragonfly

It was the size of a small hawk.

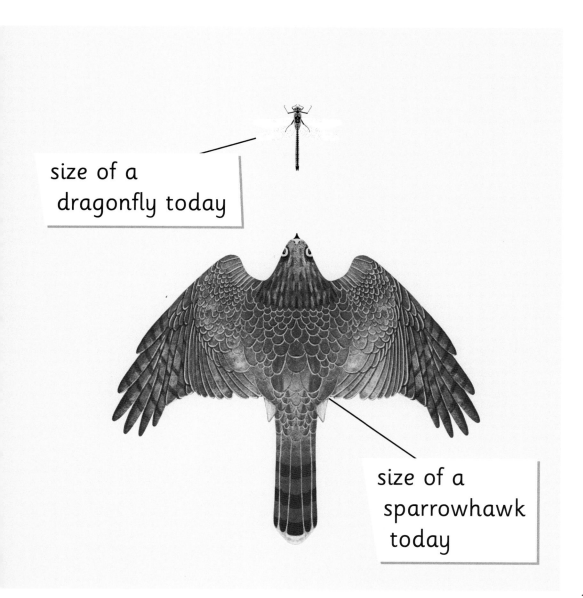

size of a
  dragonfly today

size of a
  sparrowhawk
  today

Giant millipedes roamed the forest floors.
Some were the size of your leg!

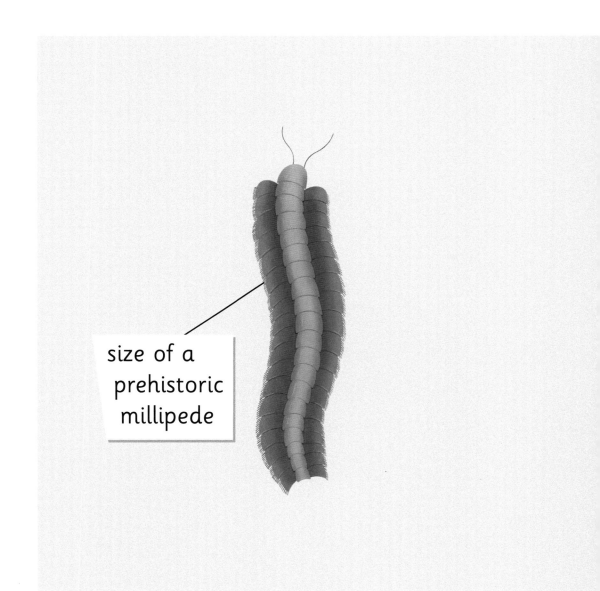

size of a
prehistoric
millipede

They ate dead leaves and seeds.

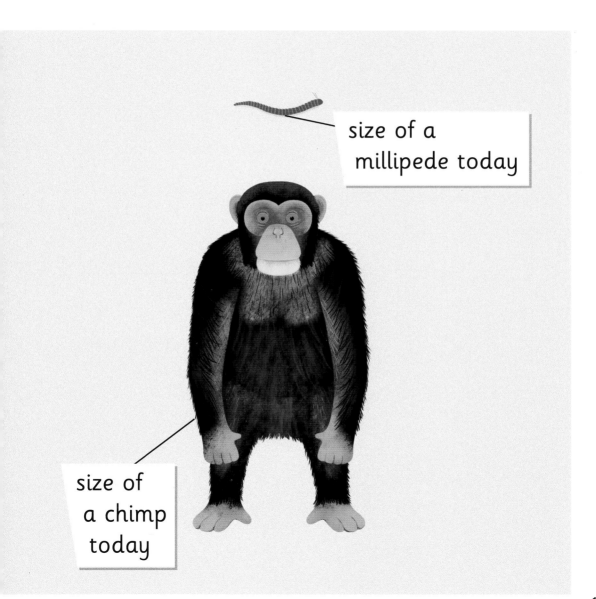

size of a
millipede today

size of
a chimp
today

Even the water was home to huge creepy crawlies.

eye stalks

sharp spikes

14

This strange prehistoric shrimp grew longer than a bike!

Long ago, even snails were super-sized.

How would you feel if you saw this snail on a seashore?

Most sea snails are herbivores.

Today, we still see millipedes, shrimp, dragonflies and snails.

They are not as big as they were before.
Why did creepy crawlies become smaller?

It's because dinosaurs became smaller. Over time, they began to fly.

Over hundreds and thousands of decades, they evolved into birds. Birds love to eat creepy crawlies!

Over time, creepy crawlies changed too. They all became smaller.

This helped them to scuttle away more quickly and hide more easily.

Next time you spot a small creepy crawly,
remember its giant relatives!